It's Fun to Choose

written by Dru Cunningham
illustrated by Richard Hackney

Library of Congress Catalog Card Number 87-91991
©1988. The STANDARD PUBLISHING Company. Cincinnati, Ohio
Division of STANDEX INTERNATIONAL Corporation. Printed in U.S.A.

Should I go barefoot,
or should I wear shoes?

If Mother doesn't tell me,
then I get to choose.

Should I go walking
or take a ride?

When Grandpa asks me,
I get to decide.

Should I eat pickles
or taste something sweet?

It's fun to choose
what I want to eat.

Should my picture be colored
with yellow or blues?

Maybe red would be better,
but I have to choose.

Should I be helpful,
or should I hide?

God hopes that we help,
but we have to decide.

Should I keep all I have
or be thoughtful and share?

God won't make me give,
but He hopes that I care.

Should I go to Jill's house
or have Joel come to play?

Mother lets me choose playmates
when I plan my day.

Should I pick up that paper
I see at my feet?

I can decide
if my world will be neat.

Should I be a doctor,
teach children, serve tea?

Someday I must decide
what I want to be.

I must choose everyday
between good things or bad.

Some choices make me happy,
but others make me sad.

Should I love God?
He said He loves me.

He hopes that I choose Him,
but He'll just wait and see.

No, I'm not a robot.
I may accept or refuse.
Yes, God really loves me
so He lets me choose.

Date Due

Code 4386-04, CLS-4, Broadman Supplies, Nashville, Tenn.,
Printed in U.S.A.